I0639385

George White

Home ballads

Devotional, Sentimental, Humorous

George White

Home ballads
Devotional, Sentimental, Humorous

ISBN/EAN: 9783744766203

Printed in Europe, USA, Canada, Australia, Japan

Cover: Foto ©Andreas Hilbeck / pixelio.de

More available books at **www.hansebooks.com**

HOME BALLADS;

DEVOTIONAL, SENTIMENTAL, HUMOROUS.

By GEO. WHITE.

CHICAGO:
MOSES WARREN, 103 STATE STREET.
1878.

4   *Contents.*

For Thy Sake.

DUTY stood at the door,
    Sternly compelling
Something that oft before
    I'd done, rebelling;
Seemed it, of all I know,
    Menial and lowly;
"Lord, should I stoop so low
    When Thou art holy?

I love the sunny sheen
    Where Thou hast led me;
Love I the pastures green,
    Where Thou hast fed me."
Just then a pleading word
    Made my weak hand shake;
And a low voice I heard—
    "Do it for my sake."

"Long have I suffered loss,
 Bearing this trial;
Carried this heavy cross
 In self-denial;
Toiled up this arduous way,
 Barren and dreary;
Lord, I would fain obey,
 But I am weary!"

"I bore the cross for thee
 Up Calvary's mountain;
Prayed in Gethsemane,
 By Kedron's fountain;
And need I urge thee still?
 Do it for My sake."
"I yield, dear Lord; I will
 Do all for Thy sake."

Love of God.

LOVE of God, so full, divine—
    It is nearer,
        It is dearer
            Far than thine.

Love of God, be more to me
    Than all other—
        Sister, brother—
            E'er could be!

Love of God, fill all my heart;
    Never, never,
        From me sever,
            Or depart!

Love of God, abide with me!
    I surrender
        Every tender
            Chord to thee.

Love of Jesus, make me whole;
 Move most sweetly,
 And completely,
  All my soul!

Love of Christ, my being nerve,
 From inertion
 To exertion,
  Thee to serve!

Love of God, endure alway;
 Ne'er grow older,
 Dimmer, colder
  Than today!

Thy Will be Done.

LORD! I would bow with Thee
In dark Gethsemane,
Praying alone.
Thou, who didst bear for me
My load of agony
In dark Gethsemane,
Thy will be done!

Bring my petition near
Into Thy heart and ear,
O holy One!
Pain darts across my way;
Thick darkness hides the day;
Yet, Lord, I still would pray,
Thy will be done!

Lord! I would go with **Thee**
Up to mount Calvary,
　　Bearing the cross;
Bearing the grief and shame
Of sundered friendship's name,
And the world's scoffs and **blame**
　　Counting but dross —

Would linger near the tree
Where Jesus died for me —
　　Died for his own:
The Father hides His face,
Darkness comes on apace,
Heaven frowns; for in disgrace
　　He dies alone.

Down to the sepulchre,
Lord! I would follow her
　　Who loved Thee well;
There, at the dawn of day,
Hear the sweet Mary say,
" Who 'll roll the stone away?"
　　Angels can tell.

"Not here!" The tidings flew;
Who died for me and you,
　　Death could not hold;
Lo! "He is risen" today,
Hear the glad angels say,
Go bear the news away—
　　The news untold.

And so my guilt is not;
This is the price that bought
　　Pardon for me;
This is the price that brings
All good and precious things,
On Faith's exultant wings,
　　Glad soul, to thee!

Faith.

FAITH is on the mountain-top;
  High above the clouds she stands,
On the Rock, and looking up,
  Hymning with the angel bands
That surround the throne of God,
Brightening His bright abode.

Lightnings play beneath her feet,
  Thunders tremble through the air,
Storms descend and torrents meet;
  Naught can hurt or harm her there;
On the Rock she firmly stands,
Hymning with the angel bands.

Though in rags she walks the streets,
  Though her couch the cold, damp ground,
Though no kindly voice doth greet,
  She hath all things and abounds;

She an heir of God and heaven —
Crowns and thrones to her are given.

And when oft the unseen Hand
  Leads her to the valley dim —
Lions chained, and devils, stand —
  Safely through she follows Him;
Through the shadows dark and gray,
Faith discerns the narrow way.

When upon the raging sea,
  Winds adverse and baffled skill,
Jesus sleeps; but waking, He
  Bids the winds and waves be still:
Gazing upward, still she stands,
Singing with the angel bands.

When the human faints and fades,
  And the mortal meets decay,
Faith escapes these narrow glades,
  Soars to ope the gates of day;
Mounting upward, still she flies
Home to God, when dying dies.

Wherefore for the Coming Day.

WHEREFORE, for the coming day,
    Care and trouble borrow?
Do thy little work today,
    Trust Him for the morrow;
Eat whate'er He gives to eat,
Trust Him for tomorrow's meat.

See thy Father's granary
    Filled to overflowing!
Jesus holds the magic key,
    Tenderly bestowing
As He willeth. Ask Him, then;
He will honored be of men.

What though weariness and pain
    Hold thy hand and waking,
The unwelcome day again
    Through the darkness breaking?

Trust Him though no work be done,
Trust at morn and set of sun.

See the lilies of the plain,
  Toiling not, nor spinning,
Knowing neither loss nor gain,
  Neither care's beginning!
Never lady, in her ease,
Was arrayed like one of these.

See the blithe birds of the air,
  Sowing not, nor reaping,
Knowing neither toil nor care—
  Flying, singing, sleeping—
Waking, praising God! why then
Are they better fed than men?

They do all they have to do,
  All that God has given;
But they murmur not, as you,
  Child and heir of Heaven;
Going where His kind hand leads,
So He warms and clothes and feeds.

Why so slow to learn of them,
  Of the birds and flowers?
Why so loth to trust in Him,
  In life's darksome hours;
We belie what we profess,
Loving little, trusting less.

Trust Him Altogether.

THROUGH foul or pleasant weather,
　　Whatever may befall,
O, trust Him altogether,
　Or trust Him not at all!
For He is fully able
　To meet thy soul's great need,
To furnish well thy table,
　And all thy hungry feed.

He giveth not by measure,
　Or grudgingly, or small;
E'en to thy faith the treasure
　Shall be proportioned all.
O, then, in stormy weather,
　Whatever may befall,
Trust in Him altogether,
　Or trust Him not at all!
What though the shadows lengthen,
　And cover all the ground;

And thy forebodings strengthen,
  As, gazing all around,
Thou viewest the ancient places,
  Where Hope has built high towers,
And over all are traces
  Of sorrow's busy hours?

Fear not! fear not! He loves thee,
  And to His loving breast,
O child of God! He holds thee,
  And there thou mayest rest.
E'en if thou fail, He loves thee,
  The clouds will break at length;
The shades are sent to prove thee,
  To try thy faith and strength!

And if thou fail not, glory
  And joy shall end thy days;
Through Jesus' strength thou'st conquered,
  To Him shall be the praise.
Then, in all stormy weather,
  Whatever may befall,
O trust Him altogether,
  Or trust Him not at all!

Star of Faith.

'TWAS a lonely waif
    Upon the sea of life,
Floating upon the tide,
    Tossing amid the strife
Of the angry, foaming billows,
    With fear and danger rife.

Borne upon the waves,
    Darkness shrouds the sky,
While fearful wind and storm
    Obey the mandate high—
It quails at the awful thunder,
    Whose lightnings round it fly.

Now the eye is fixed
    Upon a lone bright star;
Its light through darkness gleams
    Over the waves afar.

It is of heaven the token,
    Whose bright door seems ajar.

Rest, oh, troubled heart;
    List its whisperings!
'T will strength to thee impart,
    'Twill hope and courage bring,
To gain a victory mighty,
    Under a Savior King.

Safe 'twill guide thee o'er
    Life's dark, troubled sea,
Till moored on heaven's shore,
    Thy own frail bark shall be—
The gift of the dear, kind Savior,
    Sweet star of Faith to thee.

Mother.

O THE weary days of waiting
  On the borders of the river!
Days of shadow and of sadness,
Days of sunshine and of gladness,
On the heights, where past and present
Mingle with the great hereafter.

Thinking, thinking — knitting, knitting,
Little blocks of patchwork fitting,
In her old armchair a-sitting.

She's aweary and awaiting —
Weary with a life of labor,
Weary with a life of trial —
Feels her own life-work is ended;
Loving much the loving Savior,
Longs to be forever with Him;
Wonders why the summons tarries.

April with her crystal showers,
Summer with her fruits and flowers,
Autumn with his golden bowers,
Winter with his busy hours —
Years roll by, and still she ever
Hears the murmur of the river,
Sees its wavelets gleam and glisten,
Drops her work to look and listen:
One by one they 're passing over,
Still for her arrives no summons;

But her pains are growing sharper,
And her face is growing paler,
And the wrinkles something deeper;
Thinking, knitting — thinking, knitting;
Little blocks of patchwork fitting;
In her rocking-chair still sitting:

Till one day, when gentle showers
Fell upon earth's budding bowers,
Came a soft and gentle calling,
Like an angel voice at even —
All so still, we heard unheeding —

And her eyes grew brighter, brighter,
And her brow paled whiter, whiter—
Whiter than the couch she lay on—
Till a strange, mysterious glory
Filled the room and us with wonder.

Three long months in pain she lay there,
And ofttimes she talked with angels—
Often with the blessed Jesus—
Longing, longing—waiting, waiting;
Not a whit her pain abating;

But one eve, when twilight mingled
With the growing shades of darkness,
Silently and soft and welcome
Came the last and final summons.
Heaven's fragrance wafted earthward,
Light from thence illumed earth's darkness;
Earth and heaven were close together:
Then the Savior threw His mantle
Softly over her, and bare her
Safely to the realms of glory.

The River.

O VER the murmuring river,
   The loved ones are singing,
  Their melody ringing ·
Forever and ever.

Over the mystical river,
   Each knoweth the other;
   The infant, the mother,
Death cannot dissever.

Over the phantom river,
   Their pleasures are real;
   They grasp the ideal,
And hold it forever.

Over the weeping river,
   No tear of regretting,
   No sighing nor fretting,
Disturb them, forever.

Over the sleeping river,
   The heart's dearest treasures,
   The soul's sweetest pleasures,
Are waking together.

O, blessed immortals!
   That river of terror,
   The tomb of old error,
Is only heaven's portals.

The Other Side.

SHOULD I dread to cross the river,
　　Flowing darkly, deep and wide?
I shall see the Golden City
　　On the verdant heaven-side:
I shall see the holy angels,
　　Who have watched my pathway o'er;
They are waiting to convey me
　　Safely to the other shore.

I shall see my long-lost kindred,
　　And my baby-brother meet —
Father, mother, sister, hasting
　　On swift wings, their own to greet —
Not as when on earth we parted,
　　Bear they palms of victory;
And are like the blessed Jesus,
　　Clothed with immortality.

The rejected " Man of Sorrows,"
  There, methinks, I then shall see:
The exalted, glorious Savior,
  Who once walked in Galilee —
Gaze upon the loved disciple,
  Paul, and Peter, and the rest;
Greet the Marys and the Marthas,
  And the children that He blest.

I shall see the great All-Father,
  Veiled in glory, veiled in light —
Reverent angels bow their faces,
  Bow their joyous faces bright.
And the music there resounding
  Mortal ear hath never heard;
And the beauty Him surrounding
  Mortal pulse hath never stirred.

I shall view the martyred millions
  Who have died by sword and flame;
And shall see the holy prophets
  Who have loved His holy name —

Gaze with awe on untold numbers
From the islands of the sea,
From the frozen zones, the jungles,
And wild dens of Africa.

Should I dread to cross the river,
Since upon the other shore
All my treasures dear are gathered,
And my kindred gone before?
In His house, of many mansions,
Jesus hath prepared for me
A dear home: I know 'tis waiting,
And its light I long to see.

Waiting for Me.

IN a land undimmed by shadows,
   In a home where all is fair,
I have kindred waiting for me—
   Waiting my arrival there.

And methinks they stand together—
   Father, mother, gone before,
Sister, brother, kindred spirits—
   Waiting on the other shore.

And the angels, too, are kindred,
   Round the throne of God they stand;
Christ, my elder brother, waiting
   For me in His own fair land.

And the great Supreme, Eternal,
   Is my Father, and He waits
Patiently, till all His children
   Safe arrive at heaven's gates.

How the cares of earth grow lighter,
  And its pain seems less to bear,
When I feel they're waiting for me—
  Waiting my arrival there.

By-and-By.

THERE is a hope,
    There is a fear;
It may be far,
    It may be near;
But, in the future, waiting, I
Shall Jesus see; yes, by-and-by.

Impatient soul,
    And longing heart,
Your murmurs cease,
    And bear your part
Of pain and labor on life's road,
For soon 't will lead thee to thy God;

And by-and-by
    Will soon be now,
And God shall wipe
    Each tear-stained brow;

The Lamb shall feed them from His throne—
To living fountains lead His own.

O verdant fields!
O shining shore!
The Lamb of God
Spreads wide the door.
Ah, Golden City! surely I
Shall see your glories by-and-by.

Dawning.

CHRISTIAN, awake! for the daystar is dawning
That heralds the morning;
Far over the sea the nations are waking,
Their fetters are breaking;

They struggle in vain their fetters to sunder,
They struggle and wonder;
They stretch forth their hands in attitude pleading,
Oh, rest not unheeding!

Mosque and pogoda are tottering, creaking,
To you they are speaking;
The kingdom of satan is trembling, falling,
And Jesus is calling.

God by His spirit the way is preparing,
His strong arm is baring;
God in His providence wide doors is oping,
And will ye be moping?

3

Ye, who have wealth, who have intellect's power,
      What, think of the hour?
Crown it with dutiful grateful behavior;
      Give all to the Savior.

For over the world the daystar is dawning
      That heralds the morning,
And Jesus shall reign, with glad acclamations,
      The Light of all nations!

Sheltered.

MORNING dawned serenely,
    Sunlight danced around;
Birds were on the wing,
Birds were caroling;
Beautiful and seemly,
Every living thing,
Every sight and sound!

Such life's early waking;
But, e're noon was nigh,
Distant muttering,
Loud threats uttering—
Storm and thunder breaking
O'er me on swift wing—
Shelter none had I.

Through the tempest dreary,
Sped a welcome guest;

Love, upon the wing,
Unto me did sing:
Come to me, ye weary,
All your burdens bring;
I will give you rest!

Refuge I have found me
From the stormy blast—
Lo! extended wide
Jesus' arms! I hide;
Love and Peace surround me,
I will here abide
Till life's storms are past.

Galilee.

WATCHFUL angels hover round,
   O'er the heights of Galilee;
And the wondering stars look down,
   Where the Savior bends the knee.
Burdened with the guilt and scorn
   Of the world, alone, He there
Kneels, until the first faint dawn
   Of the morn, in fervent prayer.

The disciples are away
   On the raging sea below;
Winds adverse, and in dismay
   "Toiling in, they toiling row;"—
Hope and joy their bosoms thrill:
   Jesus comes! He comes! and hark!
As He utters, "Peace, be still,"
   At the port they moor their bark.

Lone disciple on life's sea,
 Frightened mariner! His love
Watcheth now, in heaven, o'er thee;
 Jesus prays for you above.
Though the waves around thee roll,
 Fear and doubt thy bosom fill,
See! He cometh to thy soul,
 On the waves, with "Peace, be still."

Mercy.

WHO, who will bear these to fallen man—
   A ruined, stubborn race?
The price of blood my Son hath shed—
   Mercy with Truth and Grace.

The spirit came—the spirit of God,
   With gifts for one and all,
Hands full of treasures rich and free,
   Many and great and small;

And softly whispers in human hearts,
   "Ask and ye shall receive;"
Ye need not hunger, need not thirst,
   Ye need not mourn and grieve:

Here's Mercy for all, both great and small;
   Repent and turn to God—
A balm to heal the wound you feel,
   Beneath His angry rod.

And Mercy still stands with open hands,
  Still waiting to bestow
Her gifts to men, the moment when
  They will to have it so.

Eye hath not seen, and ear hath not heard,
  Nor heart conceived, the bliss
Laid up above for those who love
  And follow righteousness.

Sympathy.

THERE is a sympathy
　　Above the human;
It comes alike to child,
　　To man and woman.

To high and low alike,
　　Where'er there's pining,
Or burden to be borne,
　　Or sick reclining.

And whoso'er applies,
　　However lowly,
Its soothing power feels —
　　A charm most holy.

It helps us bear our pain,
　　Our grief and sadness;
To sorrow gives again
　　The smile of gladness.

And those who stumble so,
  Their weakness showing,
It yearns to raise them up,
  With love past knowing.

This blessed sympathy,
  So freely given,
On chords of love comes down
  From God in heaven.

And in all human hearts,
  Though ill-assorted,
This godlike impulse dwells,
  But blind, distorted —

Still burning with high zeal,
  Nor scarce discerning
The true from false; for aye
  Cool reason spurning;

Yet blesses she the world,
  Through blind endeavor.
We'll clasp her to our hearts,
  For aye, forever,

And when the hot tear starts,
   We pine and languish—
We look to God above
   To sooth our anguish.

Hebrew Captives.

B Y Euphrates river, flowing
  Soft through Babylonia's street,
Sit a crowd of weary wanderers,
  Sick of heart and sore of feet.

All the way from Palestina,
  From their kindred and their home,
Driven by Chaldean masters,
  Faint and weary they have come.

On the willows by the rivers
  Hang their harps, from whose accord
Rang the praises of Jehovah,
  Only God and mighty Lord.

Mount Moriah's walls and temple,
  Fair Mount Zion's sacred keep,
And Siloam's silver waters,
  Haunt their memory — they weep.

Pitiless, the proud foe taunts them,
  Heeding not their tears and wrongs:
" Sing us one of David's measures,
  Sing us one of Zion's songs."

" Can we sing the songs of Zion,
  Can we chant Jehovah's praise,
Mid the jargon and the discord
  Of your heathen rites and ways?

We can ne'er forget thee, never,
  Never, O Jerusalem!
Be thy memory and worship
  Dearer far than diadem!

Let my hand forget her cunning,
  And my tongue in silence cleave
To my palate, if I ever
  For thy downfall cease to grieve."

So their harps hang pendent, silent,
  On the boughs by Babel's streams;—
One sweet hope, Messiah's coming,
  Through the distant future gleams.

Israel, had'st thou shunned, forsaken
Idols, revelry and sin;
Served the Lord thy God—Him only,
Oh, this never need have been!

It is Well.

TIME wings lightly, Hope is high;
  Free from care or trial,
Blest are they; and so am I—
  Blest in self-denial.

Life is pleasant, life is sweet,
  Full of joy and beauty;
Yet is my reward complete
  In the path of duty.

Life is sunshine, life is rest;
  Ease surrounds my neighbor;
Still am I supremely blest—
  Blest in toil and labor.

Plenty crowns another's days,
  Free from want or losses;
Yet am I, in all my ways,
  Blest in bearing crosses.

Though I weep while others smile,
    Knowing no aggrievement;
I mourn not, being the while
    Blest in my bereavement.

One great love encircles man,
    Yesterday, tomorrow;
And that love alike I scan,
    Both in joy and sorrow.

Satan's Pocketbook.

ROAMING with eager thought and aim,
 Unto an unknown land I came:
'T was dark and wild—I paused to look—
The murky air, the shivering gloom
Hung o'er the valley like the doom
Of banished souls; and closely by,
Borne sluggishly and silently,
The volume of a sulphurous brook.

A chain of mountains dark was seen,
Bounding the earth and Hell between;
And many of their peaks towered up
So high one could not see their top.
This awful chain of mounts was called
The mountains of God's wrath, and walled
Th' Infernal Regions in, save where
I stood; a narrow opening there

4

Was guarded well—
This gate of Hell—
By the dark image of Despair.
With eyes of fire and tongue of hate,
Prime minister of Doom he sate;
Yet chained so close he could not go
But little way from Hell, although
He guarded well th' Infernal gate.

Beyond the mountains of God's wrath,
Which walled th' Infernal Regions in,
Outstretched a landscape fair, which hath
Been singed and scorched by pain and sin;
This country fair is called the earth,
Outspreading wide a vast, vast plain,
Heaven's sunshine falling on it—
Heaven's dew and Heaven's rain;
And gazing mute, I heard, methought,
Discordant notes of music brought
Upon the wings of moving air;
And listening, I heard, I know,
The notes of joy and wail of woe
Which mingle there.

THE EARTH.

A climate where they weep and sing,
  And hearts grow colder, warmer,
With more of winter than of spring,
And more of fall than summer.

Where spectral death gloats after life,
  And storm the sunshine follows;
Contentment sweet abides with strife,
  And famine plenty swallows.

A region where the good and bad
  Grow side by side together;
Walk hand in hand, the gay and sad,
  Through foul or pleasant weather.

Where broods the raven's sable wing
  O'er love's enchanted bower;
Where lurks the serpent's fatal sting,
  Hidden beneath the flower.

A curious spot where night and morn
  By turns devour each other,
Where patience is of sorrow born
  To overcome her mother.

Lost spirits, 'scaped from prisons deep,
　Beneath where they were lying;
Work mischief with God's careless sheep,
　And lure with hope the dying.

Where prayer can drive the deel away;
　Where Pain abides with Pleasure,
Where Good and Evil strive alway
　Our hearts to rule and measure.

Where angels weep, o'er fallen man,
　Their tears of love and pity;
God's eyes, unseen, man's actions scan,
　From His Eternal City.

The air was hot, the brooklet bad
Was flowing earthward, and it had
Its scource in Hell.　Yet round and round
It zigzag coursed until it found,
Or stole, its way through Hellgate.
From Hellgate 't is Intemperance
Flows onward through earth, and thence—
A circuit wide and strange to tell—
Pours in the other side of Hell.

Alas! this stream of death and sin
Appeared to flow both out and in!
The under waters, narrow, deep,
With insidious silence creep
Over the unsuspecting world!
But on its rippling surface gleams
Delusion, and all fair it seems,
As round and round it curled.

Backward lowered a grizzly cloud,
Hovering o'er the dark abyss,
A cloud of sulphurous smoke; and loud
The devils mutter, serpents hiss—
Fearful jargon, horrid cursing,
Loud blasphemings seething, bursting,
Trembling through the turbid air,
From vengeful spirits dwelling there;
And lightning's blaze and polar night
Commingle with contending might.

Rolling, bellowing thunders sound
'Neath my feet, and shake the ground;
Their voice is heard above the din
Of demons murmuring hard within—

Within a horrid gulf, down, down,
Where ne'er a bottom hath been found.

The prisoned hissing of hell-fire,
Outbursting with a sudden ire,
Showers adown o'er all the plain
Like an ill-omened, blood-red rain,
The ashes of impure desire,
Flying upon the wings of fire;
Some sparks flew earthward, and they came
Unto the brook of sulphurous name,
And lighted on it; through the night
The passion fires gleamed lurid light,
    And sparks became
    A quenchless flame,
And war and anguish from below —
Terror, disaster, fear and woe,

And famine, desolation, pain,
Quickly spread over all the plain.
Some sparks touched buds which ne'er again
Essayed to put their beauties forth
Upon the borders of the earth;
But unto these 'twas surely given

To bud again and bloom in heaven.
Again, fire, smoke and soot flew out,
Diffusing terror all about;
And from the pit, on all around,
Were ashes strewn, and on the ground.

Dreadful eruptions! mortal fear
Embraced me, as I lingered here;
For o'er my head the mass sailed forth
That lighted on and scorched the earth.
It stayed at last; and moving fast,
I sought to 'scape this awful place;
And, musing much, I knew at last
'Twas Earth and Hell, the middle space.

Upon the margin of the brook,
And near those mountains dark and high,
Hastening past, I paused to look
At something, lost there, hard and dry;
I seized it, in my waistcoat tight
Demurely placed it, out of sight;
And saw, upon the sand and soot,
Prints of Apollyon's cloven foot;
And numerous marks there were in sight,

As though there'd been a recent fight —
He had just waged a desperate war
For some poor soul he'd bargained for.

At last I reached a quiet spot
Upon Earth's bosom, broad and fair,
And, sitting down to rest and muse
Upon my strange adventure there,
I thought upon "the something lost"
I found upon the verge of Fate;
And drew it from my waistcoat forth,
And looked it o'er as there I sate —
And sudden horrors thrilled my veins;
I dropped it, fled, then turned to look,
When there, upon the grass and soot,
Lay Satan's private Pocketbook.

O, horror upon horrors! now,
   A pretty scrape you've got into;
For devils old, and devils young,
   En masse, will soon be after you!

Why did I ever leave the Earth,
   In thought to canvass worlds unknown —

That blessed, miserable place,
  With thorns and roses overgrown?

But here I am, a helpless wight,
  Target of Chance, and sport of Fate!
O, fly thee to thy quiet home!
  A pris'ner, I; too late, too late!

For I have trespassed, trespassed deep,
  Upon forbidden ground, alone;
I cannot laugh, I cannot weep—
  My heart is like a block of stone.

The cunning chief of misery
  Is lurking near me, all unseen;
He will not lose his property
  Without one desperate grab, I ween.
Woe, woe to me! for all of life,
  Of love and hope are lost to me!
No, no! I'll give "the *deel his own*;"
  O God! thy worm appeals to Thee.

After a while, as I grew calm,
I took it up, nor felt alarm;
And slowly, without fear or hate,

Proceeded to investigate;
A still, small voice within me calmed
And bade me to unravel all
The schemes of Satan, to ensnare
Unwary ones within his thrall.

THE POCKETBOOK.

A curious thing! the outer sides,
Of adamant, could well abide
The fury of hell-fire. A bone,
Mixed with a certain kind of stone,
Inflammable, the clasp made close,
Till, from a drunkard's veins let loose,
Blood touched the spring; wide ope it flew,
With noise and crash; when to my view
Appeared the contents, lying in:
Made of a pale and haggard skin
The linings were; and diamonds rare,
And precious things, and jewels fair,
And many a price in scrip and gold,
Of fools, who e'en themselves had sold
For pleasure, to the deel for wine,
For honor, or a name to shine

On Fame's high dome. When these were past—
The price, I'll have your soul at last.

Still fumbling within, I sought
And came to one whose facts were wrought
In fiery lines, on parchment dark
As midnight, without moon or stars,
When naught Earth's quiet dreaming mars,
But soft repose her slumbers mark.
·This deed malign I leave in shade;
I cannot trace it undismayed.
Terror withstood me as I mused,
And trembling shook the hand I used.
All hastily I hurried past
The horrid details, and the last
I fain would find; but infinite
Their number seemed, and dark as night.
Hatred of sin and sinful things
Thrilled through my soul, as Satan sings,
For here laid open to my view
The hellish schemes that millions slew.
The almighty dollar, it was plain,
Had millions upon millions slain;

And many who were void of sense
Were snared and taken by "five cents."
And one whose tiny little soul
Was taken by a part or whole
Of one round cent, was detailed there;
And pennies, pennies everywhere,
And cots and palaces and towers,
And lands, dominions, thrones and powers,
And ships, and stocks, and merchandise,
Were bartered for the awful price
　　　Of human souls.

'T is strange, surprising strange, but so
He claimed dominion long ago
Of the duped Earth and all within;
Then sought a traffic to begin
With those he duped and caused to sin.
He'd fought with heaven, and, vanquished there,
Retreated backward, downward, where
He and his minions people space;
But spirits know no bound of place —
And near to Earth, too near, alas!
To Earth, from thence, in freedom pass.

'T was thus he sought to circumvent
His late discomfiture, and sent
His minions forth with title-deeds
Of lands and houses, names and creeds.

Still searching, wonders more I found,
Reclining there upon the ground—
Wonders of dark, malignant schemes, ·
Surpassing diabolic dreams
Of thought malign, and devilish plan,
To snare and conquer listless man—
Heaven's pet—for in his form and mien
The image of his God was seen.

I trembling sat in terror, pain,   . [brain;
While thought chased thought through my dazed
A loud and sudden crashing heard,
Like the collision of two worlds,
Through space careering, met at last—
The less to atoms flies, and fast
The greater moves in grandeur past.

The air now wore the murky hue
Of regions recently in view—

Of regions, I had lately flown.
A dash of vivid lightning shone,
And thunder burst and rolled around,
Then bellowed underneath the ground.
The tall trees swung their leafy arms,
And bowed low down their stalwart forms,
But did not break. The angry sky
Seemed circling to earth, and high
Of clouds sailed fragments, black as night,
In seeming terror and affright,
And dust and soot flew all about;
Flew in and out, then in and out,
And smoke of sulphur smote the sight.

But harmlessly it passed, and calm
Pervaded all around, and bright
The sun poured down a radiance warm
O'er hill, and dale, and mountain height;
The soft wind breathed a murmured prayer,
The echo murmured happiness;
And flowers bloomed in beauty there,
And stooped the soft, green earth to kiss.
The bird-song burst upon the ear,

The brooklet paused to smile and hear.
I wondered at the happy change,
So sudden, and so sweet, and strange;
And looked upon the ground in vain,
And in my pocket, in my brain;
Ah! Satan's Pocketbook had gone;
I could not wish it back again —
The devil's own — he'll have his own!

Sequel to Satan's Pocketbook.

INTEMPERANCE, swift-moving flood,
Freighted with evil, void of good—
So moved me with its ceaseless gleam,
Like a somnambulistic dream,
I climbed an elevated nook,
Where I could trace this winding brook,
To take of it another look.
The distance safe, and lofty height,
Offered an outlook, out of sight;
And lo! o'er all the prospect vast,
A strange, ill-omened light was cast,
With meaning pregnant; not a sound
Rolled through the air or jarred the ground.
I saw a noiseless little brook,
With unpretending harmless look,
Flow from beneath the portals wide
That shut close in the underside;
'Twas but a laughing little stream,
Whose merry wavelets dance and gleam,

Disclosing naught at first but joy,
To tempt with merry jokes the boy —
With gentle, soothing motion flows,
With siren measures lulling those
Who launch upon this death-bound flood.
Soon overcome with strange repose,
Or dazed with outward show of good,
Are charmed with what appeared to be
A form of loveliness and grace,
In whose voluptuous, ruddy face
Are dimpled smiles and jovial mirth,
Adorned with glittering gems of Earth.
Dancing to varied minstrelsy,
A weird, fantastic light is cast
Upon the present, future, past,
Until all solid things are made
To fall behind, and rest in shade.

The fair form changes now, and lo!
Approaching stealthily and slow,
Borne onward in a gilded bark,
Upon the waters deep and dark,
The vender of a subtle thing

5

Which makes a mortal laugh and sing,
And dance and shout e'en in death's face,
While Misery and shamed Disgrace
Hang round the bier—and yet for more
The victim wails; his honor, store,
His reputation, manhood, strength,
His bread and meat, his soul at length,
Are bartered to the deel for more.

For, just behind this vender foul,
Another stood with mince and scowl;
'Twas but a shape, though ill or fair,
With impious import hiding there,
And in his hand, with close device,
He firmly held concealed "the price;"
And cries, "'Tis naught." As on they go,
The brooklet widens; and the flow
At first is easy, with calm mien
Meanders terraced hills between,
Or softly creeps through valleys green;
But carries, with its eddies fair,
A poisoned breath, a poisoned air,
Which smites the leaf upon the trees,

And floats far off upon the breeze;
It blights the tender, budding bloom
Of gardens green with polar gloom;
It slays the grass, it slays the grain,
It stays the ever welcome rain.

The shapeless shape, holding the price,
Sulks frowningly, touches the dice;
The trifling price to any one
Looks like a little bit of fun.
Delusion; but he deftly throws
Chains over willing dupes, and goes
With even motion swiftly on,
Until, sun, moon and stars all gone,
The soul in darkness moans and quakes,
And e'en this feeble body shakes;
And the dire shape, so fair at first,
Is changed to something dark, accursed,
A horrid thing that, day and night,
Impels him on; 'tis Appetite.
The dark form rages, foams and roars,
While near a dreadful cataract pours;
A voice is heard in accents clear,

"Beware, beware, destruction's near!"
A lovely, jeweled, helping hand
Seems dropping from the better land;
It beckons to him, and implores
To turn and live. To golden shores
The hand points, bleeding; oping wide,
Light breaks the gloom and skims the tide,
And over portals deep, inwrought,
Was "touch not, taste not, handle not."
These portals led to temples fair,
Resting like jewels, here and there,
Upon earth's throbbing breast; and lo!
Many for refuge there did go,
And found the safe retreat they sought
In "touch not, taste not, handle not."

But many more rush heedless on,
'Till manhood, strength and hope are gone.
The prison houses are filled full
Of these poor wretches, bright and dull;
Proud talent meets, and wealth rests by
The sunburnt sons of poverty,
While hunger and consumption pale
List mute to disappointment's wail;

And orphans' groans,

And widows' moans,

Ambition's broken shrine, despair,

Anguish and terror, mingle there.

Rolls on the freighted flood, with power

Submerging palace, hut and tower;

Tall trees, and low,

To ruin go;

And the firm rock,

Which bore the shock

Of wind and storm for many years,

Is swept away, and naught appears

But helpless, broken fragments—e'en

Revealing what they might have been.

As round and round its waters wind,

It had whole cities undermined;

Had kings uncrowned,

And thrones borne down;

Deluged many a castle fair,

So grandly reared upon the air;

Deluged many a castle strong,

All freighted with a poet's song;

Deluged many a castle great,
Where a blazoned warrior sate;
And, wheresoe'er it winds about,
Fair homes were marred or blotted out;
And many cots of humble mien,
Or noble mansions, have been seen,
Wrecked and ruined, floating thence
On the dark stream, Intemperance—
Broad channel, ever bringing in
Victims of pleasure, vice and sin!
And o'er the bound of hell at last,
Its volume thundered full and fast.

And as they pass the fearful bourne
From whence no one can e'er return,
We hear their cries, we hear their groans,
We hear their never-ending moans;
And, as they hasten on apace,
More come to fill their vacant place—
Borne onward, as all those before,
En masse, e'en to destruction's door.
They heeded not the warning voice,
They heeded not the helping hand:

One bade them make the better choice,
One pointed to the better land.

And oh, the ghostly vision dread!
The shape ill-omened stalks ahead;
That shapeless shape, always in sight,
The fearful thing called Appetite.
The eye is riveted to it;
Will has no power to rule, or sit
Upon her ancient throne, but lies
In mute paralysis, and dies.

The lovely, jeweled hand has gone,
The day is ended, light has flown;
Now darkness reigns supreme, and all
Is merged in midnight's dismal pall;
But through the blackness backward gleam
Those horrid eyes whose glances seem
Like charm of serpent; and no light
Of cheering token breaks the night.
Near, nearer still, the cataract pours,
And from beneath loud thunder roars—
The shape, whose eyes haunt, haunt him still,
Comes nearer; with a horrid thrill,

Its finger ends but touch his brow —
He writhes, and fain would die, but now
Its lips upon his lips are pressed;
While on his eyes its eyeballs rest;
With hand to hand, and frame to frame,
They breathe as one, and are the same.
The devil has him now! The price
Was but a wicked, shrewd device,
And made to get him to this plight —
A cat's-paw of poor Appetite.
Thus Appetite bought many more
Than gold, and diamonds, and the lore
Of ancient sage, or heathen myth
Fixed up to treat the season with.
But over all Earthland shone bright
Cities of refuge, clean and white,
With temples rising to the sky,
Imprinted on whose portals high,
And visible in every spot,
Was "touch not, taste not, handle not."

And many millions more are near
The cataract; some devoid of fear —

So stupefied their senses are,
They see no danger, near or far,
While just ahead the torrent roars,
And over hell's high walls it pours;

But other some, more millions told,
Know all, hear all and all behold,
Of danger and destruction nigh;
They struggle with their chains, and try
With might and main the spell to break;
But no, with senses wide awake,
They hasten on, for Appetite
Has fangs upon them close and tight.

In vain they struggle, strive in vain,
To break the spell, to burst the chain;
Cities of refuge all are passed,
The helping hand is gone at last;
On hurrying to their dreaful fate —
Poor souls, poor souls! it is too late!
You would not heed the golden hand,
You would not list the warning voice:
One pointed to the better land,
One bade you make the better choice;

One pointed to fair cities forth,
Which sit like jewels on the earth,
On whose high portals, deep inwrought,
Was "touch not, taste not, handle not."

Polly Hone.

O NCE an old crone
   Lived all alone;
Her name was simply Polly Hone.

Her sister dead,
Her brother led
A wandering life. She never wed.

Her neighbors proud,
She thought, aloud;
Some better ones to find, she vowed;

And vainly thought
There surely ought
Somewhere to be a better spot.

The truth to own,
Poor Polly Hone
Disliked to live so much alone.

So one day she
Resolved to be
A traveler, and the world to see.

Too much, of late,
She 'd heard folks prate
Of a new town in a new State.

This town out west,
She thought it best
To seek; its name was Cozynest.

Said she, "The keers,
For one of years,
Have many breakdowns, horrors, fears.

'T will give me time,
And be sublime,
To go by Foot & Walker's line."

So, firm in mind,
New scenes to find,
She looked around, and felt resigned.

Then leave she took
Of vale and brook,
Of quiet home — a cosy nook;

But, when set out
Upon her route,
Found many things to whine about:

The wind was cold,
Her garments old,
The road had mud and mire untold.

Still, fully bent
On her intent,
She traveled on, nor did relent.

Day after day
She jogged away,
And never stopped to rest or pray,

Till, nearly through
Her route so new,
Tired out, she knew not what to do;

Her appetite,
As well it might,
Loud clamoring for food that night;

To take some rest
She thought it best,
Ere she arrived at Cozynest.

A farmhouse lay
Just on her way,
With lawn and garden green and gay;

The door in sight
Seemed to invite,
With open arms, this wayworn wight.

Admittance sought,
Just as she ought,
Her rap at length an answer brought.

A matron came, ·
(Her much I blame)
To see a woman old and lame,

Whose feet were sore,
As at the door
With staff and scrip she stood before.

"Please, let me stay
Tonight, I pray;
To Cozynest I'm on my way."

"I have no taste
For vagrants — haste;
A tavern lies beyond the waste;"

And, pointing o'er
A cold, bleak moor,
Upon the woman closed the door

Poor Polly Hone
Stood there alone;
Then in a moment more had gone,

The sun was low;
The wind raved so,
She must needs stop to pant and blow.

The setting sun
Had now begun
To warn home trav'lers, one by one,

But, when at last
The day had past,
Darkness she saw approaching fast.

Cold hung the night;
The stars blinked bright
At Polly Hone in her sad plight.

Poor Polly Hone
Would almost own
She'd rather be at home alone.

At last a light
Appeared in sight,
Cheerfully shining through the night.

Expectant, she
Walked eagerly,
Longing to grasp the "is to be";

She soon drew near
To a small, queer
And dingy-looking house; with fear

Her knees did quake;
She trembling spake
To one who stood there, half awake

And half asleep:
"Pray, do you keep
A tavern here, in this droll heap?"

"Yes, ma'am; I do;
And good fare, too;
And room enough for likes o' you."

And glad was she
A place to see,
Though poor, where yet some rest might be.

A supper queer
Was served her here —
Potatoes, cabbage, bread and beer.

When past, "a bed
I'd like," she said,
"On which to lay my weary head."

Then she was led
Unto a bed
Of straw; and she was mad, she said,

And made a vow
She'd "raise a row,
Before she'd pay 'em, anyhow."

But sleep at last
Her eyelids fast
Sealed up, and bright dreams o'er her cast.

Soon morning light
Shone clear and bright,
And woke her to her piteous plight.

Her cloak, anon,
She then put on,
And, e'er they knew it, she had gone.

Soon Cozynest,
Away out west,
Gleamed on her sight—a place of rest.

No steeple there,
The house of prayer
To mark—nor here, nor anywhere;

And, looking round
Awhile, she found
Not much there to be seen but ground.

A prairie wide
Stretched on one side,
On th' other great burr-oaks abide;

So strange and new,
She stopped to view
The river slowly winding through.

Too slow, too slow
Its waters flow!
No pebbles on its banks so low!

And then at last
She stood aghast,
To see the people move so fast.

The houses low,
All in a row —
Some things too fast, and some too slow.

At length, the day
Wearing away,
She thought to find a place to stay —

"Stop, ye ole croon;
I 'll hev yer, soon;
Ye 've bothered me from morn till noon."

And looking back,
Close on her track
Her landlord came with all his pack.

In blank dismay,
She could not say
One word; said he "I want my pay —

"Twelve shillings, mum;
Hand over! come,
Or the police 'ill give ye some."

Too late, too late!
The magistrate
Of Cozynest was there in state.

Ah, well! thought she,
I'll pay my fee,
Then from annoyance I'll be free.

The fee was paid;
Still undismayed,
She mused until her plan was laid.

A house to find,
She had in mind,
Where she could live content, resigned.

But such hard luck
Had killed her pluck —
Worried her brain; and there she stuck,

Almost distraught.
At length she thought,
To make one effort more, I ought;

And so, once more,
From door to door,
All Cozynest she traversed o'er.

It did befall
No house at all
To sell or rent, nor large, nor small.

So in a huff
She took some snuff,
And thought she'd seen the world enough.

The homeward track,
With staff and pack,
She took again, and traveled back.

Once home again,
She thought it vain
To seek to flee from care and pain.

And, wiser grown,
She lives alone,
Content to be poor Polly Hone.

She sings away,
The livelong day;
Now list to what her song doth say:

"Though friends have flown,
And cares have grown,
Be wise—let well enough alone;

For it is plain
That, all in vain,
We seek for sunshine in the rain;

But, after rain,

We look again,

And sunshine dances o'er the plain.

And all things wait,

At Heaven's Gate,

For pearls that never come too late.

But on the wise,

In deep disguise,

They fall like raindrops from the skies.

So, after rain,

We look again,

And pearldrops gleam upon the plain."

Human Sympathy.

ONCE, on a certain time,
    I fell to dreaming;
The day was in decline—
    A twilight seeming.

When in the dimness, lo!
    A great crowd hovered
Upon an even plain,
    Completely covered.

A crowd promiscuous,
    Of all sorts, gathered:
The blind, the lame, the halt,
    The old and withered.

The young, the rich, the poor,
    The tall, the meagre;
And each one waiting there,
    Expectant, eager.

And each a burden bore,
  Though well or ailing—
'Twas large, or small, as each
  Could bear unfailing:

When suddenly appeared
  A light most holy;
From far above it came,
  Descending slowly,

Till when, short space above
  The crowd it hovered,
One wearing human form
  Could be discovered;

A form of lovely mien,
  A maiden seeming,
With pity, o'er the throng,
  Her mild eye beaming.

Poised low in air, above
  The crowd she lingers;
While pity issues from
  Her eyes, her fingers.

To mitigate life's ills,
    Her chief concernment;
While on her brow was traced
    "Want of discernment."

And thus, at length, she spake,
    The silence breaking:
"I came from heaven to soothe
    And cure your aching;

Will linger here awhile —
    For many morrows;
Then come! I have a balm
    For all your sorrows."

A millionaire came first —
    At which I wondered —
Who in a recent fire
    Had lost "five hundred;"

The loss he seemed to feel
    Keenly, intensely;
The sympathy he craved,
    He got immensely.

An old man next advanced;
　　His head was hoary;
In trembling accents he
　　Told his sad story.

A little balm he got,
　　His grief abating,
And then was thrust aside
　　For others waiting.

A maiden—pale and worn
　　With constant tending
Upon a mother sick,
　　And slowly bending

Beneath the weight of years
　　And constant ailing—
For Human Sympathy
　　Came, unavailing.

A lady, sweet and sad,
　　Beneath her hovered;
There, dressed in sable garb,
　　Her grief uncovered:

Two lovely infants lay
　As though they slumbered;
They died while yet their age
　In months was numbered.

A manly form laid low
　Beneath the willow;
She'd shared with him his cares,
　His bread, his pillow.

Into her heart and ear
　Comfort distilling,
Came Sympathy, her own
　True mission filling.

A poor man next appeared,
　With reason shattered;
'Twas plain the gutter had
　His clothes bespattered;

Yet gentle Sympathy
　But one look gave him;
And would not raise her soft,
　White hand to save him.

A lady, on whose face
 Was spread her trouble,
Now told her thrilling tale:
 Her corns were double;

And, sometimes it would seem,
 Her head ached badly;
And of her aches and pains
 She murmured sadly.

A generous slice she got,
 If I saw plainly,
And still her business seemed
 To murmur, mainly.

The blind, the lame, the poor,
 All helter-skelter,
Next clamored on the stage
 For food and shelter;

Some food and shelter found;
 Some but a meagre
Award of sympathy,
 Altho' so eager;

And some got kicks and cuffs,
   And maledictions;
I wondered, in my dream,
   At these distinctions.

The drunkard's children came
   To gain the treasure;
To each she gave a small
   And stinted measure.

The orphans next applied —
   And there were many;
To some she gave full weight,
   To some, not any.

This whole transaction was
   So farce-like seeming,
I groaned, and rubbed my eyes,
   And woke from dreaming.

Circumstance vs. Providence.

CREATED things were new;
    God, in his grace, made Good,
And sat her in her place—
A presence fair to view.
Then Evil came out from
The nothingness of space—
Admiring, sought to wed,
Persistent, though she fled
In haste his hateful form.

At last she came to earth;
Wearied she lighted there;
Lusting, he followed her,
O'ercame her by a snare;
Usurped her right of birth,
And marred the things that **were.**

Of Good and Evil born
Was one, named Circumstance:

She lay on earth forlorn;
Men came and called her chance.
God pitied when he saw,
And gave to Circumstance.
The realms of Earth—not Chance,
Or arbitrary Law.

One came and died for man,
One bruiséd Evil's head;
Evil became as dead;
His doom was written then.
Of Evil, all that came
Were doomed—e'en Circumstance;
And her misnomer, Chance,
Was known no more by name.

Thence towers a mystic plan,
Majestic, broad and high;
Its arms encircle Earth,
Its head is in the sky;
Law is the outside part,
But Law is not the heart;
By it God governs still,
Through it He works His will,
All wise and good, and makes

Law rule the elements,
And nothing jars or breaks.
For God controls the springs
That work such wondrous things
To human sight and sense —
Its name is Providence.

Men cannot understand,
It is so broad and high;
They see no head or hand,
And so the whole deny.
Through it God will restore
To Good her rightful sway;
Evil shall be no more —
Like night, 'twill pass away
When morn's bright rays are seen;
And Good shall be Earth's queen.
Bide patiently and wait,
It will not come "too late."

Grace and May.

SWEET little Grace, with her winning face,
    And her eyes so full of glee—
Of the household all, both great and small,
    The pet and the darling, she.

Poor little May is homely, they say,
    But good, and gentle, and mild;
She blushes that she was born to be
    A drunkard's poor little child.

Beautiful Grace, with smiles on her face,
    And love in her soft, brown eye,
Runs to the gate to frolic and wait,
    And kiss dear papa good-bye.

Poor little May, all the livelong day,
    Murmurs, nor falters, nor lags;
The baby she tends, the stockings mends,
    And sews up the carpet-rags.

7

Frolicsome Grace wears curls, with a trace
    Of mirth in her mouth and eye,
She's pictures and books, a doll that looks
    Like a fay, and dolls that cry.

Pensively May sits sewing away,
    But happy enough for that;
She owns no toy, but gazes with joy
    At the pranks of her small cat.

Happy is Grace; she has a large place
    In hearts both loving and true;
She hears kind words, like chirping of birds,
    And words of good counsel, too.

Pity poor May: she hears all the day
    Discord, and jarring, and strife;
No kind words greet with melody sweet
    The dawn of her frail young life.

A pitying eye looks from on high —
    That pitying name is Love;
All, all is well; He calls her to dwell
    With Him and angels above.

Ida.

M ARCH winds shake the window pane,
Chase the clouds and bear the rain;
Pause, and their commotion cease,
For the hour fore-shadows Peace.

Lo! the setting sun, at last,
Hues of red and amber cast
O'er the clouds; and overhead
Gleams a fair fantastic red—
Throws a gleam of promise round,
Over tree, and roof, and ground,
And the cottage window where
Lay a mother, pale and fair;
Little angel baby sweet,
Sunshine comes, your birth to greet;
Wind and storm their tumult cease,
For the hour is one of Peace.

Mother looks into her eyes,
Opening with glad surprise—

Eyes of deep and mellow blue —
Reading them as mothers do;
Joyfully essayed to speak,
Answering, and kissed her cheek.

Little golden angel, where
Did you lose your wings so fair?
Glad am I they dropped today,
So you cannot fly away;
Now you're mine to have and keep,
Mine awake and mine asleep;
Babyhood and girlhood mine,
Mine in womanhood to shine —
Wondrous beauty, born for fame,
Peerless Ida is your name.

Ida crowed, and smiled, and grew,
Day by day, as babies do;
Tiny hands and tiny feet,
Dimpled cheeks, and lips so sweet;
Light brown hair with tinge of red,
Curled in cues all o'er her head;
Wept, and slept, and dreamed, and smiled —
Beautiful, precocious child.

High of brow and pale of cheek,
Mother watched from week to week —
Woke and watched both night and day,
Watched her sleep and watched her play;
Soothed her infantile distress —
Love dispelling weariness.

But the autumn time, at last,
Over earth his mantle cast —
Gay of color, cold of breath;
Lo! the obvious import Death.

Death! But oh! he loves the fair;
Loves the pure and spotless, rare;
Loves the good, and loves the wise;
Loves the ones we love and prize.
Ida died. A mother's love
Could not shield her baby dove
From Death's chilling touch. How meek
Mother's love! how strong, how weak!
Give Death all he asks, 'tis vain
To remonstrate in your pain.

Ida dead! a tiny rose,
Fallen off at even's close,

Sweetly yielded up her breath,
More than beautiful in death;
Like a smitten cherub lay
In her coffin, cold as clay;
Like a pure and precious gem,
Worn in seraph's diadem,
Falling jarred, bewildered, chilled;
So, a little grave was filled.

Friends were there to sympathize
With the mother — with surprise
Saw her face so pale and white —
Then laid Ida out of sight.

Then the mother softly stepped,
Stood and looked, but never wept;
How her purposes were crossed —
Ida dead and Ida lost!
All was gone, the world a blank!
None to love and none to thank!
All her plans of future bliss
Blown to atoms! worse than this,
Ida in some dreadful place,
With companions vile and base!

Dreams of terror and of pain
Fretted her disordered brain;
So her sisters came and said,
She is crazed, or out of head.

Ida's mother silence kept—
Pined and paled, but never wept;
Missed the burden from her arms,
Missed her winning baby charms,
Missed her cunning, artless grace,
Missed her little dimpled face:
Tried to pray; but prayer was caught
In the wings of roving thought;
And oft times she feared the Lord
Had forgotten His kind word;
Thought, if He remembered her,
'Twas with hate for sins that were:
Thus we judge the Almighty's plan
By the littleness of man.

How the mother longed to see
Baby as she used to be!
Or of her to get a glance,
In a dream or in a trance;

Murmured, prayed, and then she wept,
Prayed again, and softly slept:
Dreamed? or was it really so?
Answer, mothers, you that know.
Lo! a radiant form divine,
Being's essence full, divine,
Fount of love and Love's own Name,
To the mother's bedside came;
Presence peerless! Overawed
Mother lay, for It was God.

In His loving arms He bore
Ida as she was before—
Ida as she used to be;
But more beautiful was she;
Far more blessed, sweet and fair
Looked she, as she nestled there.
Mother did not speak or stir,
Or attempt to get at her;
Evermore she could resign
Her to Being so divine.

Jesus spake, and to her said:
In my arms your babe is laid;

I, the Shepherd of the sheep,
Do your tender lambkin keep—
Take her from your arms, but from
Evil that would swiftly come;
Take her from your sight, to raise
You to higher thoughts and ways;
And prevent you clinging so
To the perishing below.
Do not judge Jehovah's plan
By the deeds of puny man;
But resign her to My love,
And your lost one find above;
For I hold your baby, blest,
Safe within my loving breast;
She shall always here remain,
Free from sin, secure from pain.

The Snow-Storm.

A CLOUD of snow, one cold winter's day,
  Wrapped in the halo of sunset, lay
Nestling dreamily there alone
In the golden light where the sun went down,
Till stars shone out, and the moon rose high
Up to the top of the azure sky.

Then it crept around, till close in among
The specks of light where the pole-star hung,
And slept till northern lights danced so high
They touched the moon in the top of the sky;
Then it rolled itself up in a sable vest,
And dreamed till the moon had gone to rest.

At last, when aurora's finger-tips
Touched the brow of the eastern hills,
Silently opening eyes and lips,
The dome above with her mantle fills;
Then did the waiting snow-storm espy
The chariot of storm-king coming nigh,
So they join hands, and away they fly.

Far over the hills and lofty mounts,
And over the vales and frozen founts,
By the halls of the rich, and cots of the poor,
They piled the snow up high at each door;
Then over the fields and gardens fair,
Over a little grave, cold and bare;
Then storm-king paused, and his soul was stirred,
For a baby's voice from the grave he heard.

"Moldering deep in the grave I sleep,
And mamma weeps as the cold winds creep
Through chinks in her humble cottage door,
While the cold storm wildly surges o'er.
O, beautiful snow! she loved me well;
And you, so pure, alone, can I tell
How papa came home so crazed one night
With rum, he shut out ma from my sight;
And I, the baby, was left alone
To weep or sleep on the cold hearth-stone.
He then sank down on the floor, and slept,
And I to my papa's side close crept,
With mamma shut out in the cold, cold storm;
I lay there wondering, still and warm —

Too still and warm, for something close press'd
Over my head and over my breast:
And so I died; for papa lay on
And smothered to death his little son.
With a burning tear ma buried me here,
And I thought, as you came so close and near,
And your soft, white hand so gently press'd,
O, beautiful snow! on my cold, cold breast,
I'd tell it to you; and now you know,
Beautiful, beautiful, cold, white snow!"

Mournfully sighing, sadly and slow,
The cold wind warmed into murmurs low;
And the drifting snow above the main,
Melting to tears, descended like rain —
Wept o'er the ignorant, wise and witty,
Wept o'er the hamlet, the town and city,
Wept over forest, mountain and plain,
Plentiful showers of cold, cold rain;
Then ceased.

I Wish.

I WISH I had a little house,
    A little parlor in it;
I wish I had a pie to make,
    I'd hasten to begin it.

I wish I had an organ, and
    An everlasting play-day;
I wish I had a silk dress on,
    Then I should be a lady.

I wish I had a ship at sea,
    Loaded with silks and laces,
Six costly shawls, and tapestry —
    About a hundred cases.

I wish I had a bookcase stout,
    Of little books and big books;
A river full of pike and trout,
    And "forty-'leven" fish-hooks.

I wish I had a shiny day,
    Around a great, big mountain;
I wish I was a girl at play
    Beside a splashing fountain.

I wish I had a somebody
    To worry and to tease me;
I wish I had a bumble-bee,
    I'd let him buzz to please me.

I wish I had ten thousand pounds,
    And half a pound of candy;
I wish I had a small greyhound,
    And cat to fight him, handy.

I wish I had a ruby lip,
    Like two red, mellow cherries;
I wish I had two eyes to look
    Just like two huckleberries.

I wish I had a horse and shay,
    I'd make a celebration,
And take a ride, some pleasant day,
    Over the wide creation.

I wish I had some stout wings made;
  I'd fly up to the moon, and
Investigate its light and shade,
  Some pleasant night in June; and—

I wish I had a telescope,
  To sweep the constellations;
I wish I had a key to ope
  Some strange hallucinations.

I wish—I wish—I wish—I wish—
  I wish I was a poet;
I wish I had a new hat—I
  Would go somewhere to show it.

Woman's Rights.

PLEASE listen, ye croakers and praters!
  Who gabble of women and Rights,
As though we were made to hoe 'taters,
  Or mix in political fights.

Your way through the crowd you can elbow,
  You delicate lady, to vote;
Your dutiful husband remaining
  At home, "just to mend up his coat."

On 'lection day make us a stump-speech,
  Make money, make love, and flour;
When Jeff raises Ned, raise an army,
  And fight for your country and power.

Or shovel your way to the stable,
  On a bright, cold wintry day,
To put on the harness and bridle,
  And hitch up old Bob to the sleigh;

Ride over to pretty young Maister's,
 And ask if he pleases to go
A sleighing, this beautiful morning,
 Far over the beautiful snow.

And then, if he deigns to say "yes, ma'am,"
 You boost him so gracefully in,
The buffalo robes tuck about him,
 Close up to his whiskers and chin.

Scrape off all the snow from your small feet,
 And get in the other side;
Then take up the whip and the bridle,
 And so swiftly away you glide.

O! what upon earth are you thinking
 And a driving at, all your lives?
You may gather bushels of honey,
 If you don't tip over the hives.

Pray, let the world be as God made it;
 Let the masculines still be men;
Let them build all the railroads they can,
 You can "boss" as to where and when.

Broad fields now lie open before you:—
  Home, colleges, clerkships and pen;
Avail you of all, if you please to,
  But, oh! don't you try to be men.

The World in Antithesis.

'TIS a good and a bad world,
 A world old and new;
A happy and sad world,
 A world false and true.

'Tis a large and a small world,
 A silent and loud;
A heavy and light world
 Of sunshine and cloud.

'Tis a slow and a fast world,
 'Tis dark and 'tis light;
It is mystical, plain,
 'Tis black and 'tis white.

'Tis a wet and a dry world,
 Unlovely and fair;
A selfishly just world,
 A common and rare.

'Tis a rich and a poor world,
  A foolish and wise;
A noble and mean world
  Of plausible lies.

'Tis a bitter and sweet world—
  A kiss and a blow;
A noisy and still world,
  A friend and a foe.

'Tis a strange and a queer world;
  'Tis haughty and meek;
A long and a short world;
  'Tis strong and 'tis weak.

'Tis a tender and tough world;
  'Tis crooked and straight;
A pure and a vile world
  Of love and of hate.

'Tis a jovial and sad world,
  'Tis gay and 'tis grave;
'Tis sober and drunken,
  A master and slave.

'Tis a crazy and sane world,
  'Tis dirty and clean;
'Tis idle, 'tis busy,
  'Tis fat and 'tis lean.

It is lavish and stingy,
  'Tis hungry and full;
A hot and a cold world,
  A lively and dull.

'Tis a smooth and a rough world,
  'Tis cruel and kind;
'Tis civilized, savage,
  'Tis rough and refined.

'Tis a high and a low world,
  The meanest and best;
A noisy and calm world
  Of labor and rest.

'Tis a blest and a curst world,
  Thoughtful and thoughtless;
  A right and a wrong world,
  Faulty and faultless.

'T is a half and a whole world;
  Real and seeming,
A rested and tired world,
  Doing and dreaming.

'T is an honored, despised world;
  It walks and it rides,
It crawls and it flies with
  The winds and the tides;

And it goes with a jingle
  By water and steam;
'T is made up of pickles,
  And candy, and cream.

It is broad at the front and
  Contracted behind;
'T is genial, friendly,
  'T is cold and unkind.

'T is a talkative, dumb world,
  Serious and vain;
A strangely mixed-up world
  Of pleasure and pain.

Men and Women.

A LIFETIME it takes you men to get rich,
    And, when you get rich, you die;—
Better spread your energies doing good,
    And laying up stores on high.

There is only one coin that is current **above,**
    One Bank that will never fail;
That coin you can get upon earth — 'tis **Love,**
    And the bank is beyond the vale.

Ye love to gather you silver and gold,
    And houses and lands so fair;
What loss, should the water and fire sweep all,
    If you have a mansion there?

It takes you women a lifetime of toil
    To follow the style, and flirt;
Better spend your energies doing good,
    Or mending your husband's shirt.

There is only one style where you go at last —
　　One style for the rich and poor!
And the hearse is waiting for all of us —
　　It may be close to our door.

Ye love to gather you jewels and gold
　　Of curious, rare device;
Should you own no glittering gem, what loss,
　　If you have the Pearl of Price.

Fair women! your elegant styles are vain;
　　Your bodies will turn to dust;
And men, the treasures you've piled so high
　　Will soon be consumed by rust.

Take a medium — for the Irishman said
　　"There is a middle extrame"—
Not hurry and worry for wealth and style —
　　For a useless, idle dream.

But, oh! there are treasures that never fade —
　　One style, and that style is love;
The orders are *filled* in this world of ours,
　　And they will be *cashed* above.

Song of the Wind.

I COME from the mystical zones of earth—
  The banqueting halls of Thunder;
From the cradle of storm, with noise and mirth,
  I mount up with joy and wonder;
I blow, and I blow, and carry the snow,
  Piling it higher and higher,
As hither I come, and thither I go,
  Crazy with mirth or ire.

Then I scale the hilltops towering high,
  I scale the loftiest mountain;
I scale the dumb clouds, and I touch the sky,
  And play with the flowing fountain;
I·moan with pain, and I carry the rain
  Down to the slumbering city,
And I patter and pour on roof and door,
  In anger or in pity.

I kiss the wet sand on the sweet seaside,
  And launch on the tranquil ocean;
I goad her bosom to anger, and ride
  On Terror amid commotion;
I baffle the ships that are out at sea,
  I plague the mariner toiling;
And tumble their freight of humanity
  Into the ocean boiling.

I carry the clouds, all blackened with death,
  And hurricane on my shoulder;—
I moan through the gorge with abated breath,
  And carve my name on the boulder;
I blow their houses out into the street,
  I toy with trees of the wildwood;
And carry, wherever my forces meet,
  Terror to age and childhood.

I pause and blow, breathing softly and slow,
  Over fields of grain and clover;
Sweet odors I bring on feathery wing
  To the maiden and her lover.
But I come from the mystical zones of earth,
  The banqueting halls of Thunder;
The cradle of Storm with music and mirth
  I rise and fly from under.

Sunshine.

GREET the golden sunshine,
  Blessing as it flies,
Silently and swiftly,
  From the cloudless skies;
Like the vale of heaven,
  Mystically bright,
Fluttering to earthward,
  Dissipates the night.

Falling like a blessing
  On the leaf and flower;
Lifting up the dew-drop
  From the summer bower;
Wakes the joy of morning,
  Wakes the happy bird;
Harmony and gladness
  Everywhere are heard.

Shine, oh! shine upon us,
  Till all discords cease,

And the earth reposes
    In the arms of Peace!
Shine! oh, shine in splendor
    From thy throne above,
Till the earth is circled
    In the arms of Love!

Then shine on, forever,
    And forever still!
Haste to do the bidding
    Of thy Maker's will,
Haste to bless His creatures,
    As thou hast before,
And shine on forever,
    And forever more!

Angels' Visits.

A DREAM.

DO they watch, and do they wait
   For the weal of mortals?
Do they come from heaven's gate
   E'en to death's dim portals?
Do the angels visit men
   When all things confuse us?
Do they come to help us when
   Friends mistake, misuse us?

Slumber deep the eyelids close,
   Welcome to the weary;
Tired nature could repose,
   Though the night hung dreary;
Thought alone was wakeful, still
   Would escape the prisoned
Mysteries that would flit and thrill
   Through the brain bedizened.

Then anon the darkness sped,
  For a light was dawning;
Through the room a radiance shed,
  Brighter far than morning;
And a form beside me stood —
  Beautiful, undying —
Pinions poised, as though he would
  Soon to heaven be flying.

As I held the open word,
  Trembling, half affrighted,
How my very soul was stirred,
  Comforted, delighted!
Hands immortal, unconstrained,
  Traced each verse most sweetly,
And immortal tongue explained
  All to me completely.

Drink, my soul! thy fill of light —
  Drink thy fill of pleasure!
Grasp the sacred boon tonight —
  Grasp the golden treasure!
But the vision tarries not,
  Shadows round me gather;
Darkness broods; I was, methought,
  Dreaming altogether.

Guardian Angels.

"Are they not all ministering spirits, sent forth to minister for those who shall be heirs of salvation?"—*Paul.*

SPIRITS are light, and oft repose
  On piles of sunset clouds at even,
Or, poised in air, their pinions close,
  A space midway 'twixt earth and heaven.

There, whether good or whether bad,
  Sent, albeit, by God or devil,
They lure us, and we follow glad
  The path we choose, for good or evil.

When sickness, pain or death appears,
  The good ones ever round us hover—
Shield us from danger, wipe our tears,
  Our couch of pain their kind wings cover.

They soothe our grief; guard our repose;
  They wait for us at heaven's portal,
Thence sent to minister to those
  Who shall be heirs of life immortal.

And oft, when Evil throws his darts,
   With thought malign, so thick around us,
Their gentle breathings touch our hearts,
   Their own soft wings, forsooth, surround us.

And stronger grow the chords that bind
   Our willing souls to the Supernal,
While Hope exults, and Faith entwines
   Around us arms of Love eternal.

And when, at last, the touch of Death
   From fear of Sin or sinning frees us,
In arms of Love, on wings of Faith,
   They bear our happy souls to Jesus.

Sonnet.

IN vain we seek on earth to find
 A place adapted to our mind;
There's trouble here, annoyance there,
And inconvenience everywhere;
While blessings that are so mixed up
With pain in every human cup
Are overlooked, or scarce discerned,
Sometimes despised, or madly spurned,
Like some abominated thing;
And so away on magic wing
They fly. And, when they're half forgot,
We stop, and ponder, and relent,
And recognize their kind intent,
And would recall them, but cannot.

9

Deferred.

GHOSTS of the past! They're buried; let them
I would not resurrect them, or deny   [lie;
But that "it might have been" in days gone by.

'T is over, now; and patiently I wait
Who comes to welcome me at heaven's gate,
And claim me for his own true spirit's mate.

And yet, I miss the genial light that shone
From kindred eyes, so fond, into my own—
Miss the strong arm, and grope along alone.

Yet not alone; for lo! a cheering ray
Shines o'er my path. God knoweth still my way,
And angels chant to me from day to day.

'T is better thus to be, than to be wed
To one whose eye congenial light has fled—
The shadow of affection cold and dead;

Or to a drunkard, knave, or fool, or all
Combined in one. Forsooth, Fear's carnival
Would hold strange revel prone beneath Hate's pall.

So may it be. The good Lord keep, I pray,
Our blighted buds, until in heaven's day
They put forth bloom that ne'er shall fade away.

Love.

LOVE is most divinely fair;
  Love will live forever —
Azure eyes and golden hair,
  Changing never, never.
Oh, my Love, thou art divine
  Essence pure of heaven;
Never rapture such as mine
  Unto mortal given!

But my Love is dead, is dead;
  Wrap him in a shadow;
Smooth a pillow for his head
  In the silent meadow.
Cease my heart to thrill, to thrill,
  Break not with your sorrow;
Love is Love, immortal still,
  Love will rise tomorrow!

Color.

.

COLOR is beauty, and beauty
 Sits on the leaf and flower,
Clothing the trees of the forest,
 Draping the summer bower.

Seeking the hills and the valleys,
 The fields and the gardens fair;
Touching them in her gladness,
 She traces her image there.

Fair green is the dearest color
 God to nature has given;
But green is only a shadow
 Of verdant hills in heaven.

Red loves the tulips and roses,
 Red is the color of love;
But red is only the token
 Of perfected hues above.

The yellow that gilds the sunset
  Light and beauty has given,
Is only a faded picture
  Of brighter scenes in heaven.

Tomorrow our eyes will open,
  And the clod will fall away;
New tints then shall gild the dawning
  Of a never-ending day.

www.ingramcontent.com/pod-product-compliance
Lightning Source LLC
Chambersburg PA
CBHW020408030726
47496CB00007B/2361